MAYBE YOU HAD TO BE THERE, BY DUNCAN

**MAYBE YOU HAD TO BE THERE, BY DUNCAN**

*Published by*
Polestar Press Ltd., R.R. 1, Winlaw, B.C., V0G 2J0, 226-7670
*Distributed by*
Raincoast Books, 112 East 3rd Avenue, Vancouver, B.C.,
V5T 1C8, 604-873-6581
*Canadian Cataloguing in Publication Data*

Cover and interior illustrations by San Mitchell

*To my children, Kai and Rebecca, who continue to en-
lighten, encourage and enchant me, and to my parents,
Ruth and Eugene Hartley, for their lifeling example and
support, this book is lovingly dedicated.*

# MAYBE YOU HAD TO BE THERE, BY DUNCAN

## SUE ANN ALDERSON

POLESTAR
BOOK PUBLISHERS

Dear Mrs. Trumbley,

I know my novel is late and it was due last Tuesday, but if you read it, it sort of explains why I couldn't get it done on time and maybe you will accept it anyway. I hope so.

You know how you told our class to write out of our own experience, about things we know? Like you said not to write about Africa unless we'd been there? Well, this is a novel about my own family and my friend Magnolia and what happened when....but I don't want to give away the whole story now or you won't enjoy it, Mrs. Trumbley. The main thing I want to say is: *This is a true story.*

Your friend,

*Duncan*

P.S. If this novel seems a little hard to believe in places, well, maybe you had to be there.

# 1

I, Duncan, used to lead the average humdrum daily life of a male-type kid, Grade Seven, North America, Earth, Galaxy, The Universe. I sent away for free catalogues about computerized solar-powered spy equipment. I watched T.V. I lifted weights in secret. I read books about Gandhi and non-violence. I wished I had a more reasonable name, like Mike or Sport or Binky. From time to time I worried about nuclear war, what I was going to write for English class, and when my voice was going to change. I watched T.V. It was an ordinary life. The kind I thought everyone lived. Until I met Magnolia.

I met Magnolia by accident on April Fool's Day. It was her first day at our school. I wouldn't have noticed her probably, if it weren't for the baked beans. She had long dark hair and horn-rimmed glasses, and she wasn't a bit tricked out like a lot of the girls. She carried her lunch and books and stuff in an old canvas backpack that looked like it had gone through World War I in the Sahara. And that's where she kept her thermos. The thermos she asked old Hoskins to open.

Hoskins is our school's bully. Every school needs a bully, to teach kids about the Real World. Otherwise, we could go through life thinking people were okay. Hoskins must have studied up on bullying every minute of his spare time, because he'd been through ten schools by the time he got to ours. Rumour had it he'd thrown a kid out of a window in the last one. I believed it. Hoskins was one mean kid.

So on April first when he was bilking protection money out of two six-year-olds during recess and this new girl walked right up to him and asked him to help open her thermos, I had to watch. Anything could happen. Hoskins wasn't likely to mug her on the playground, but he could accidentally break her glasses, or at the very least, her thermos. She needed someone to warn her about staying away from Hoskins and I figured I was elected. I also figured I'd wait 'til Hoskins was at a safe distance before I warned her. So I stood there, watching.

Darned if Hoskins wasn't so surprised by Magnolia that he just took the thermos and started to twist the top. It was obviously stuck on tight because it took him quite a while. Finally, though, he did it, and holy galoshes! As soon as he broke the suction, there was this loud pop and dark little things flew up out of the thermos and all over Hoskins — his hair, his face, his jacket. He dropped the thermos.

"Baked beans," said Magnolia, picking up the thermos. "A couple of weeks old. They'll do it every time. Could I have the lid back? Thanks."

Hoskins was so flabbergasted he just handed her the lid and stood there for a minute while the two Grade Ones took off, laughing like crazy. Then Hoskins went inside to clean himself off before anyone else could see him looking ridiculous.

This girl, I thought, is one brave kid. I wondered if I could ever be that brave — brave enough to stand up to Hoskins on my own. I doubted it. But I knew I wanted to get to know Magnolia better, so I went over to her.

"I just want to tell you," I said, "that was swell. Do you do that kind of stuff a lot?"

"Not a lot," she said. "Sometimes. What's your name?"

"Binky," I said. That's not my name but it seemed a good one to give at the time.

"Mine's Magnolia," she said. "Stay away from that guy Hoskins. He's a creep."

"Right," I said, "I will."

"Doing anything after school?" Magnolia asked.

"Not much," I said.

"I'm going down by the Pitch 'n Putt at the beach. Want to come?"

"Sure," I said. "What do you do there?"

"Watch for flying golf balls," Magnolia said seriously. "Like the sign says."

I knew the sign she was talking about.

"Sounds good," I said.

"Sounds goofy," Magnolia corrected me with a smile, "but it works."

☆ ☆ ☆ ☆ ☆ ☆ ☆

After school we walked down to the beach and waited around under the "Watch for Flying Golf Balls" sign. The sun was out and brilliant, more like June than April.

"What's your real name, Binky?" Magnolia asked.

"Promise not to laugh?"

"I promise."

"It's Duncan."

11

Magnolia didn't laugh. She was shading her eyes from the brightness and scanning the shrubs.

"There it is," she said. She walked a few steps and bent to pick something up.

It was a golf ball with little pink wings taped on. On the ball was written in purple ink, "Water's edge."

"Come on," she said, heading for the beach. The tide was going out. We walked down to where the beach sand turned darker.

"You look that way," she said. "I'll go this way."

"What are we looking for?"

"I'm not sure. You'll know if you find it." And she headed off away from me, scanning the sand, walking around logs, briefly exploring crevices under big rocks.

I figured I'd get the hang of it doing the same in the opposite direction. Pretty soon I found it tucked among the roots of what must have once been a fair size tree. It was a small blue bottle, corked, with a note inside.

"I found it!" I yelled at Magnolia's back, jogging toward her. She turned and jogged to meet me half-way.

I uncorked the bottle and took out the note. In the same purple ink, it said: "Museum park, 3 p.m. — S.A.M."

"Thanks for finding it," Magnolia said tucking the note into her backpack. "You can have the bottle."

It was a fine bottle — you could tell it was old from the bubbles in the glass, and blue is my favourite.

"Thanks," I said, and then, as casually as I could

make it, "You wouldn't want to tell me what's going on, would you?"

"I thought you'd never ask," she said. "It's from Harold, Lord Earl of Dorcestor. He's my dad. It means the battle is on for tomorrow. Want to come?"

"The battle?"

"Not a real one. A medieval one. S.A.M. means Society for Amateur Medievalists. It's a sort of club for people interested in the Middle Ages. Tomorrow we're staging the Battle of Hastings — you know, in 1066 when the Normans conquered the Saxons and William I became King of England? It's like a play — want to come?"

"Sure," I said. Why not? The next day would be Saturday. What did I have better to do than go to a medieval battle?

Of course there was the novel I had to write for you, Mrs. Trumbley. I'd been putting it off for two weeks and it was due on Tuesday, but I didn't know what to write about. Maybe I'd get some ideas at the battle.

Magnolia explained more on the way home. It turned out she'd moved in a block away from my house. Her parents belonged to S.A.M. and so did she. They created their own characters and studied up on the Middle Ages and got together every now and then for a tournament, or to recreate a famous battle. There were little groups like these all over the world, Magnolia said, and they elected a new King every year because the King had to travel all over the world visiting his shires. It was just too exhausting and expensive to be King for more than one year at a time nowadays.

"Why the golf ball and the bottle?" I asked, feeling in my pocket for my lucky name-tag key-chain. It was missing. I must have left it at home.

"Just a quirk," she said. "It makes it more interesting. Here's where I live. See you tomorrow?"

"Sure," I said. "Magnolia?"

She was half way up the walk. "Yeah?"

"It was nice meeting you."

"It was nice meeting you too, Duncan. Call me Maggie."

"Sure thing, Maggie," I said. "Bye!"

She waved and went in.

# 2

When I got home, my mom was stripping paint off an old wooden chair in the driveway. This was her hobby, taking the paint off old wooden chairs. She uses this chemical stuff that smells awful and it's a mess getting the paint off, but the chairs do look pretty good after.

We have a basement full of old wooden chairs. Mom picks them up everywhere — second hand stores, flea markets, garage sales. Nothing makes her happier than finding another old chair loaded with twenty layers of paint to scrape off.

Under the paint she often finds the original designs — flowers, leaves, vines or little hearts. Once she found one with little birds and she was tickled for months.

She never buys them already stripped in antique stores, of course. That wouldn't be half as interesting. Sometimes she finds one missing a seat or a leg and she seems especially fond of those. "Chair abuse," she'll mutter as she fixes it.

She'll spend weeks fixing a broken one up and then pack it carefully away in the basement with the others. I bet I'm the only kid in the neighbourhood whose mother keeps two hundred old chairs in the basement. She could probably sell them and get a lot of money for them, but she doesn't because, as she says, "I wouldn't want them to go to a bad home. I'd worry."

The chairs are a bit embarrassing, but otherwise she's a pretty normal mom. She thinks about my future a lot — things like what I'll be and who I'll marry and how tall I'll grow. And she doesn't get off on cooking much. She'd rather scrape paint. Which is fine with me, because she cooks frozen food most of the time, and I happen to love a lot of things they've got frozen now.

"Spaghetti for supper," she said as I came up the walk. "Go on in. It's ready."

I was amazed. Spaghetti is one thing you can't get

frozen, so we only have it on special occasions.

"Is it your birthday?" I asked. "Or Dad's?"

"It's a surprise. I'll let your dad tell you when he's ready to — it's his surprise. Go on in now."

Mom washed up and followed me in; Dad served up the spaghetti. I waited all during dinner to hear the surprise, but Dad was curiously quiet.

"Well, tell us about school," Mom asked as usual at 6:15 sharp every night during supper. "Anything interesting happen?"

"Nope," I said as usual at 6:16 every night. "Have to write a novel by Tuesday."

"Oh, that's nice, dear," Mom said, not listening. I couldn't figure out what was going on. Both she and Dad seemed to be thinking about something else so hard they were scarcely there.

"I think I'll write it about a kid whose mother has a nervous breakdown, ends up in a mental hospital and finally kills herself," I said.

"That's nice, dear," said Mom.

"I think I'll make his father into a big time gangster who beats him and kills people and is finally electrocuted," I continued.

"That's nice, dear," said Mom.

"You should be careful with electricity," said Dad. "With that, you don't fool around."

"Right," I said. "Anyway, this kid is on his own after his parents are dead."

"That's too bad, dear," said Mom.

"And he has to find out the family secret because there *is* a family secret and his parents went to their graves not telling him." I was trying to be subtle.

"He'll just have to be patient," said my mother. She's not so dumb.

"Patience is a virtue," said my dad.

"Patience," I said, "may be the root of all evil."

"I thought that was selfishness," said Mom.

"No," said Dad, "it's money."

"The spaghetti is good," I said.

"That's nice, dear," said Mom.

Two hours later I still didn't know what the surprise was.

Finally, I couldn't take it any longer. I walked into the living room where Mom and Dad were sitting reading and said, "Excuse me, but if somebody does not tell me what Dad's surprise is, the reason for that magnificent feast of spaghetti tonight, I will go beserk, eat every chair in the basement and then shinny up the drain pipe and jump off the roof, thereby commit-ting suicide and making a mess of the driveway."

"You don't have to be so theatrical," said my mom. "Quiet good taste is better every time."

"All right," said my dad. "I'll tell you. It's a little

18

premature, but I'll tell you. Just remember, this is a secret. Don't tell anybody.''

"I swear," I said.

"Well. You know how I've been working with Eddie on his holography table?''

Sure I knew. By day, Dad and his buddy Eddie were dentists. By night they were holographers. Dad and Eddie had built a table in Eddie's basement next door, and they spent most of their spare time there. Dad would have built a table in our basement, but the chairs took up all the room. Dad and Eddie fooled around with lasers — Eddie had enough money to buy this kind of stuff, but he wasn't as smart as Dad when it came to figuring out how to use it. They actually had made a couple of pretty good holograms.

"So that's it!" I said. "Did you make hologram number three? Can I see it?''

"Not quite," said Dad. "You see, we were trying to holograph a pineapple and we decided to get creative and aimed the lasers and pressed the buttons a whole different way, and for new lengths of time, to see if that would work better, and what do you think happened?''

"The hologram came out over-exposed?'' I guessed. It was the only logical thing I could think of, but it didn't explain the spaghetti celebration.

"No, the hologram didn't come out at all," Dad said with a triumphant gleam in his eye. "The pineapple disappeared.''

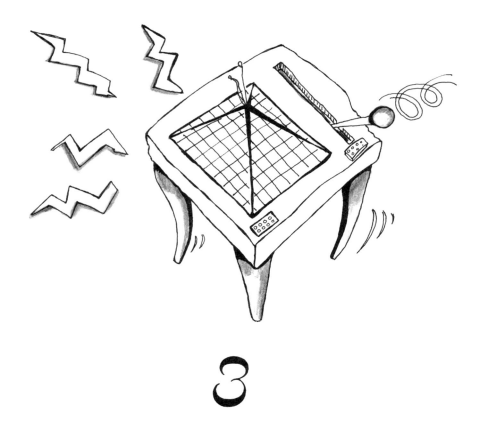

# 3

"It was an accident," Dad had gone on to explain. "We weren't trying to dematerialize it. It just happened. We're not even really sure how we did it. And we don't know how to rematerialize it, that's for sure."

"But where did it go?" I asked.

"Who knows? Toronto? Tanzania? It could be anywhere. Maybe back in time, even. Or forwards, the Future. This is big stuff, Duncan. No one understands it. As far as we know, we are the first to successfully dematerialize anything. A real break-through.''

''Did you look under the table?'' I asked. ''Maybe it just fell off.''

''We looked,'' said Dad. ''We looked.''

I went to bed with my head full of dematerializing pineapples and thought about my dad-the-dentist, now a famous holographer. It was a break-through all right. If they could figure out how to dematerialize nuclear weapons, they could ensure world peace. There was no end to practical applications. Instead of pulling teeth, they could zap the tooth and it would disappear. As long as they didn't disappear the person.

Then it hit me. Such an important secret would make my dad the target for every criminal and government conspiracy in the world. In fact, none of us would be safe. Mom and I could be kidnapped and the ransom would be the secret of dematerializing, and then we'd all be killed so whoever got the secret would have absolute power. I have an active imagination, except when it comes to writing novels, Mrs. Trumbley.

I knew I was panicking. Keep calm, I told myself. Dad and Eddie don't even know how they did it. Maybe they'll never find out — it could have been a once-in-a-lifetime thing. So far, no one knows but us and Eddie. Keep it like that.

''It's got to be a secret,'' I told my dad at breakfast.

''What has?''

22

"The pineapple. Otherwise we'll all be killed."

"Don't be paranoid," said my dad. "It was only a pineapple."

"Duncan has a point," said my mom, popping frozen papaya fritters in the toaster. "The world may not be ready. Tell Eddie to keep it a secret."

"Okay, okay, it's a secret. No one would believe it anyway," said Dad. "It was only a pineapple. Not even ripe yet."

"It might be ripe when it comes back," said Mom.

"If it comes back," said Dad.

Dad was right — no one would believe it anyway. I hadn't thought about that. It was a great comfort to me, and I was feeling really relaxed when I got to the battlefield at the museum at two-thirty.

The museum grounds were full of people, some of them audience, some of them looking for an audience.

I could see medieval tents in the middle of the ground, but since I was early, I decided to walk around the edges a bit before looking for Magnolia.

Small, innocent-looking children were playing cheerfully:

"Bang, bang, you're dead!"

"No, I'm not, I have a heliatron shield on!"

"You're dead! I zapped you with my laser gun!"

"Lasers can't go through heliatron!"

"I zapped you in your runners. They're not heliatron!"

"I have magic feet! They bounce the lasers back to you. You're the dead one!"

I like to watch little kids working things out.

I moved on. I bought an ice cream cone from a health foods vendor who handed out a leaflet with every cone. The leaflet said the ice cream was entirely natural and healthy, having no chemicals, artificial ingredients, sugar or cream in it.

Somebody sitting under a tree was playing a guitar. Several people stood around him, three of them wearing those radio-headphone gizmos over their ears. The ones wearing head-gear were bobbing and twitching to a hard rock beat. The guitarist was singing "Greensleeves," an old folksong. I strolled on.

From a branch of another tree hung a dulcimer. Near it, I was a bit surprised to see Dad's pal Eddie sitting cross-legged with one eye closed, as if he were meditating half-way. Eddie is on the peculiar side, if you ask me. He has bushy bright red hair, which I happen to like, and he flosses a lot, which I find hard to understand. He has two rather weird collections. He collects ancient dental tools that look like implements of torture. And he collects teeth — all kinds. Baby teeth, gorilla teeth, every tooth he's ever pulled. His prize possession is a copy of Einstein's teeth. He always looks at me as if he'd like to add a tooth

THE TOOTH OF SAINT ANTHONY

of mine to his collection, but Dad says take no notice. The most suspicious thing about Eddie is that Hoskins, the school bully, is his nephew. Dad says Eddie can't help that.

My dad has got to be the most trusting man on earth. Unlike Eddie, he has short curly hair and he only flosses when my mom reminds him. Anyway, I didn't know Eddie was into meditation and dulcimers, but I wasn't that surprised to see him at the scene of a battle. When he goes to school Sports Days, he's the one yelling, "Go on, Hoskins, KILL, KILL, KILL!"

I was going to say "Hi" to Eddie when a little kid walked up to the dulcimer and reached up to pat it. "Don't touch!" yelled Eddie. "If you touch that, your fingers will turn purple and drop off!"

The little kid ran away. I decided to skip talking to Eddie.

Then Hoskins appeared carrying a ghetto blaster. He switched it on and the loudest rock music I've ever heard crashed over the park like a tidal wave. It sounded like someone revving a motor cycle while playing a chain saw. To my amazement, Hoskins and Eddie started break-dancing — or trying to. They couldn't really do it — mostly Eddie jumped around and Hoskins shadow-boxed the dulcimer. Then a small crowd started moving towards them shouting "Quiet!" and "Turn it off!" Hoskins made a face but he switched off the music and left. Eddie went back to meditating. I moved on.

Two middle-aged joggers, a man and a woman, passed me. I could hear the man saying, between puffs, "And the greatest horse of all...was Man-o'War..."

"What happened to him, dear?" asked the woman.

"He broke every record there was...."

"Did he have a tape-deck?"

I couldn't hear the man's answer.

The little kids were playing off to one side. "I'm the King of the castle and you're a dirty rascal...."

In another area, a clown was doing his act, surrounded by a small crowd. I couldn't see through or over the crowd enough to see the act, but it was fun watching an old couple at the outer edge. They each had a small French poodle. The couple were short, so they couldn't see anything either, but they were holding their dogs up on their shoulders so the dogs could see. It was a peaceful crowd.

The medievalists were camped in the centre of the grounds, the Normans clustered around a purple tent with fancy velvet banners, and the Saxons clumped around a rough burlap tent. They had banners too, but they were plainer.

I didn't remember Magnolia saying which side she was on, so I kept moving back and forth, looking. The men wore heavy chain mail from head to foot, and the women wore medieval dresses — long skirts, flowing sleeves. It was like being in the middle of a movie set. I looked carefully at every girl I passed, but none of them was Magnolia.

"Out of my way! Watch it!" Maggie's voice came from behind me, and I jumped to one side and turned, but there were only three knights in armour carrying a bale of hay.

"Maggie?" I asked tentatively. Was she a ventriloquist?

"Over here," said one of the knights. "Grab hold and give us a hand, will you? This thing is heavy!"

I grabbed the hay and we carried it to the centre of the area between the two camps.

"I didn't recognize you," I said to Maggie, the knight in front of me.

"Probably didn't expect me to be in armour," she said. "Didn't know there were maiden warriors in the Middle Ages, did you?"

"No, I didn't."

"Well, there were a few, and I'm one. Beats embroidering tapestries. You can be my squire if you want."

"Okay. How do you get to be a knight?"

"Start as a squire and work your way up. Study, practice, go on quests, do brave and honourable deeds, be loyal and faithful. You know, the usual."

I thought I might like to be a knight, but it sounded like it would take a long time. However, I'd be on the look-out for quests, starting now.

We lugged around a dozen bales of hay to form the bridge for the battle, and then Maggie got me out-

28

fitted in some homespun breeches and a loose shirt.

"When the battle starts, keep back," she said. "Without armour you can get a broken bone from an accidental blow from a mace. Your job is to get me back on my feet if I fall — this chain mail is too heavy for me to get up fast by myself.''

We'd been sitting around the Saxon tent. Inside, Magnolia's mother, Matilde-the-Fair, was busy telling a group of kids and their parents about S.A.M. Magnolia's dad, the Lord Harold, was practicing juggling.

We could see tour buses pulling up in front of the museum, but the tourists filed inside. They didn't come back to watch.

''Something special going on in there?'' I asked.

''A travelling exhibit,'' she explained. ''Of medieval stuff — this is their opening day. That's why we're holding this battle — it sort of all goes together. They've got all kinds of armour and utensils in there, and they're supposed to have one of the stranger medieval relics — the Church wasn't sure if it was real or not, so it's one of those relics some people took seriously and some didn't.''

''What kind of relic is it?''

''It's called the Tooth of Saint Anthony of Padua.''

''A tooth? Have you seen it?''

''Not yet — too busy setting up. Want to go after the battle?''

''Sure. When's it going to start, anyway?''

''About now.''

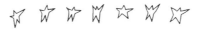

The battle was terrific. The Saxons massed on one side of the hay, and the Normans on the other, and someone blew a horn, and they charged each other. The women and kids stayed back and cheered, rooting for their side. The knights parried blows, their armour clanging and bonking. The chain mail was made from bed springs and flashed in the sun.

The rule was, if you got hit between the knee and the shoulder, you had to declare yourself dead. Head-hitting wasn't allowed. They wore helmets and face pieces, but it would still have been too dangerous. The battle didn't last long, and Magnolia was in there for most of it. She didn't fall, but she finally got killed by a blow above the knee and joined me on the side-lines. When the horn blew again, marking the end of the battle, she was laughing hysterically.

"The wrong side won," she explained. "We'll have to do it again and give the Normans another chance to beat us. Otherwise, English history is in big trouble."

So they re-ran the battle, and this time the Saxons held back and the Normans won. Maybe that's the way it really happened anyway. The second time, Harold's leg was broken by a blow from a mace. Maybe fighting is dumb even when the armour is neat. Harold had to go to the hospital for a cast. I decided I didn't want to be a knight after all.

31

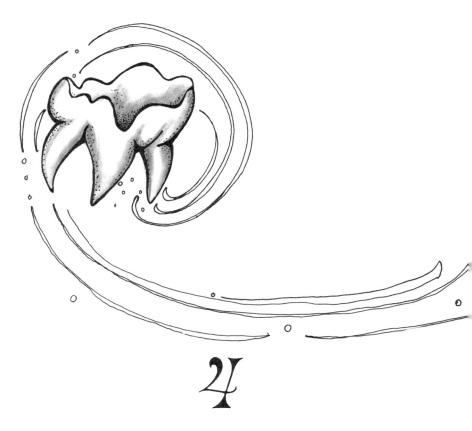

## 4

It wasn't time for the feast yet — all S.A.M. battles ended in a feast — so Magnolia got out of her armour and we went inside the museum to look at the exhibit.

There was a huge crowd around the case holding the tooth. I'd expected that, but the crowd was in a kind of disturbed hubbub that didn't seem normal at all. As we got closer, we could make out fragments: "It's gone... I can't see... Maybe they didn't put it

in yet?... No... Nothing else touched... Stolen?...
Must be ..."

Magnolia and I wormed our way through the crowd.
Kids like us can do that. You just bend your knees to
look as little as possible and say, "Excuse me," and
shoulder through. People move aside automatically.

As we got closer to the glass case, the tone of the
crowd changed — there was laughing and people were
saying things like, "A joke, it's some kind of joke...
What a sense of humour.... Must be a stunt for a T.V.
show...."

Finally, Magnolia and I reached the display case in
the middle of the throng. There, sitting swathed in
white velvet behind a card printed with the words,
"Relic: Alleged Tooth of Saint Anthony of Padua,"
was a slightly green pineapple. As if that weren't
bad enough, hooked on to one green spike at the top
was my lucky key-chain name-tag, there for all the
world to see, saying "Duncan."

"Duncan?" Magnolia said thoughtfully. "A pineapple
named Duncan?"

"Call me Binky," I whispered. "Excuse me, I've
got to make a phone call."

Luckily, Dad was home when I called.

"I think I found your pineapple," I said.

"That's wonderful," said Dad. "Where?"

"You wouldn't believe it," I said. "I'll tell you later.
Dad, how come you didn't mention my name-tag?"

"I forgot," he said. "We were trying for special

effects — art holography — a fruit with a name. You know. So, you found your name-tag too? That's wonderful!"

"Wonderful," I said. "The only problem is, it's locked with the pineapple in a display case in the museum for the whole world to see, and it's in the place of the Tooth of Saint Anthony which seems to have entirely disappeared. The tooth wouldn't happen to be in Eddie's basement, would it? It could have fallen under the table."

"I'll look," said Dad. "I told you, the technique is not perfected yet. These things take time. I'll look."

We rejoined the medievalists to help set up for the feast only to discover a new set of problems. They had long wooden trestle tables readied with wooden bowls and goblets for mead, and they'd been planning to cook a gigantic fish over an open fire. They'd brought the fish, packed in ice, in one of the member's trucks, and had prepared a fire on the beach. But, of course, when the fire was ready, the fish had disappeared.

"Anyone could have taken it," sighed Magnolia's mum, Matilde-the-Fair.

"Was the truck locked?" I asked.

"Yes, but even a five-year-old knows how to pick a lock nowadays," said Matilde.

"I mean, was the truck locked when you went to get the fish?"

"Come to think of it, yes. Now why would a fish-thief lock the truck back up?"

"Excuse me," I said. "I have to make a phone call."

"Dad?"

"Yes?"

"When you were looking for the tooth, did you press any of the buttons?"

"As a matter of fact, I did. To see if I could get the pineapple back."

"Your setting must have been a bit off. You disappeared a fish."

"Really? Oh, that *is* interesting. What kind of fish?"

"A dead one."

"Humm. Less interesting. Where was it?"

"In a locked truck."

"How is the truck?"

"The truck is fine."

"Well, that *is* good news! That means two times I've done it — the tooth from a locked case inside the museum, and the fish from a locked truck. It's a break-through for sure — better than Houdini. If I could only figure out how I did it..."

"Do me a favour, Dad. Don't press any more buttons — at least not until we get this thing sorted out. Be careful."

"Duncan, in this life you want to live with one foot in the future. You've got to have heart — you have to risk, you have to gamble — do you think Edison discovered the steam shovel by being careful?"

"No, Dad. I don't think he did."

"You see? Trust me."

"Oh well," said Magnolia to her mother when I came back from the phone booth, "Binky and I can hop a bus over to the market if it's still open and buy another fish."

"It's going to rain," said Matilde-the-Fair.

"We'll wear raingear," said Magnolia, who had changed out of her armour. She took two plastic raincoats and two pairs of boots from the costume trunk and gave me one set, a very large one.

"On we go to the market," I said. "It may be closed, but in this life you have to take risks. You have to gamble."

Magnolia gave me a funny look and we started

across the grounds to the bus stop.

The market was mostly closed when we got there, but one fish stand was open. A woman was packing it up.

"Want a bargain on a nice fish?" she asked. "End of the day bargain, $2.25 for this fish as big as you are! I don't know where it came from — suddenly it was just here. My last fish — do you want it?"

I never could resist a bargain. The fish was huge, almost as long as I am tall, and heavy. Magnolia and I carried it between us back to the bus stop and a bus was waiting, but when the driver saw us with this enormous fish, he closed the doors in a hurry and drove away. No heart.

"Maybe he was afraid the fish would smell," said Magnolia.

"Help me button it inside the raincoat," I said. "Otherwise we could be here all night."

The driver had been right. The fish did smell.

I must have looked a bit strange, all lumps inside this raincoat so long on me it dragged on the ground, but the next bus driver let us on anyway. The bus was almost empty, except for two women sitting together towards the front.

We sat a few seats behind them. When they talked they weren't especially quiet.

"Kids!" said one.

"Yah! Kids!" said the other.

"Dressing up. They like to fool around."

"Yah, dress-ups. My kids too, I remember. Always dress-ups!"

Then one tried to whisper.

"Did you notice his tail?" she said.

"Yah. I did. Poor kid. A think like that could ruin your life."

"Hardships are made to overcome," said the first. "He'll be a better person for it."

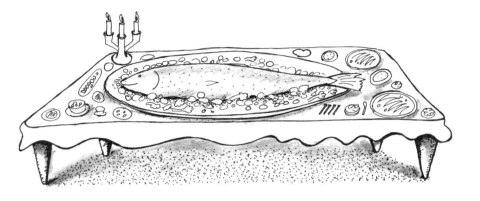

# 5

Back at the medieval feast, Matilde was delighted to see the fish, and set to work cleaning it immediately. First she scaled it. Then she gutted it. Then she screamed.

Magnolia and I looked where she was pointing. In the opened stomach of the fish was an enormous tooth.

"It's okay," I said, scooping the tooth into my

pocket. "I'll take care of this. Don't give it another thought."

"I'm sorry I screamed," said Matilde-the-Fair. "It caught me by surprise."

"Of course," I said. "I would have screamed too."

"Kids!" said Matilde-the-Fair, and she went back to preparing the fish.

I called Dad.

"I found the tooth in a fish," I said, "and I want you to promise me you'll keep your hands off those buttons, at least for tonight, while I figure out how to get the tooth back inside the museum."

"Was it the same fish?"

"I don't know — I think so. What difference does it make?"

"It could be another break-through!"

"Dad. Please!"

"Okay. Okay."

The feast was magnificent — the fish, potatoes, chestnuts, a roast, even mead. I only tasted the mead — I don't want to get into heavy drinking, medieval or not. Your average Hoskins would probably have gone whole hog, but for me, a little mead goes a long way. Especially when I have to put a tooth back inside a locked case inside a museum, a guarded museum. Since the discovery of the pineapple named Duncan exchanged for the Tooth of Saint Anthony, the museum security force had been reinforced with police patrols.

After dinner, I called home to tell Mom and Dad not to wait up for me — I said I was having a fine time with the medievalists and that Magnolia's mom had invited me to sleep on the couch at Magnolia's house if we were getting back very late.

"That's nice dear," said Mom. "Have a good time."

Magnolia told her folks she and I had decided to go for a walk and then bus home — they should go along in their car and not worry about her — the night was young and the buses irregular. She might be in late.

"All right," said Matilde-the-Fair. "It's Sunday tomorrow. You can sleep in."

☆ ☆ ☆ ☆ ☆ ☆ ☆

I slipped into the museum just before closing time. I had to hide until everyone was gone so I could return the tooth to its case. Magnolia waited for me out front. We agreed to whistle if there was any trouble.

I found a door marked "No Entry" and tried the knob. It opened. After a set of stairs, I was in an attic full of the most amazing curiosities — a mounted moose head, Chinese jars, Indian baskets, a harpsi-

chord, antique sewing machines and shoes, masks from New Guinea, fishnets, kerosene lamps and endless crates and boxes. I waited. I heard the closing bell and waited a lot longer. Finally, I tiptoed back down to the main floor. I opened the door a crack and looked for guards, but the hall was empty.

I crept from case to case, trying to be as unobtrusive as possiblein case a patrol came through, and I'd almost made it to the pineapple, when I heard a series of creaks and, finally, what sounded much like a loud yawn. I cowered under a case containing jewelry and looked in the direction of the sound.

It was coming from a standing suit of armour.

Oh, good, I thought. Sleepy ghosts. That's all I need.

There was another yawn and a couple of clanks. I noticed a dust pan on the floor neatly lined up with the feet of the sleepy suit of armour. Then I noticed that the suit was holding in its right hand a push broom. Maybe I was in the presence of a medieval janitor's ghost.

Suddenly, the left arm moved up. I held my breath. The glove went to the visor and pushed it up, over the crest of the helmet. A face? Yes. I didn't know whether this was good or bad. Then the ghost spoke.

''You, there, under the table. Give me a hand out of this suit. If you don't tell I was napping on the job, I won't tell anybody you're breaking the regulations.''

The ghost sounded real enough.

I helped him out of his armour.

"Thanks," he said. "Now if you all will leave quietly by the side door, the police in front won't ask what you're doing in the museum after closing."

I started when the janitor said "you all," but when I followed his gaze, it made sense. Across the room, looking at a case of old manuscripts, were Eddie and his horrible nephew, Hoskins. They pretended not to hear.

"I mean you with the hair and your sidekick, too," said the janitor. "You must have missed the closing bell."

"I'm a little deaf," said Eddie. "Hello, young Duncan. This is a strange place for you to be at night."

"Yes, sir, I'm meeting a friend," I said, hoping that would be answer enough. I wondered if Hoskins would get me in a headlock when we got outside and Eddie would yell, "Kill, kill, kill" until he made me tell about finding the tooth in the fish. He already knew about the pineapple, of course, and I wondered if he was trying to get it back too. But I couldn't figure out why he would do that. There *are* more pineapples around, and he didn't collect name-tags.

The janitor showed us out. It was completely dark and the museum grounds were deserted. The sky was now clear and I could see the Big Dipper and Venus. I whistled Magnolia's signal, trying to look unconcerned, and started walking away toward the bus stop when Hoskins grabbed my arm and said, "Hold it, buster."

"I want a little talk with you," Eddie began. "I had a chat with your dad and it seems you have found something I would dearly like you have."

"Oh yeah?" Play for time, I thought. I whistled.

"The tooth," he said. "I know you have the tooth of Saint Anthony. I want that tooth. For my collection, you know. It means a great deal to me, and it can't mean very much to you. What could a kid do with a tooth? I'll give you ten bucks for it."

I thought. I could get myself out of trouble here by giving him the tooth. It was tempting. It would be cowardly and dishonest because the tooth didn't belong to me, it belonged to the museum collection and should be there for everybody to see, not locked away with Eddie's tooth collection. But I am not known for my bravery and Hoskins was starting to twist my arm.

On the other hand, if I gave him the tooth, would that be the end of it? No, I wouldn't feel right until the tooth was returned. Could I give him the tooth now and call the police later? No, they probably wouldn't believe me. And if they did, the story would be out; there'd be newspaper stories and everyone would know about Dad's talents at holography. That would not be safe. (I'm only telling you about this, Mrs. Trumbley, because I know you will keep this novel secret. What a student writes for a teacher is confidential, isn't it? Besides, if Eddie could tell a goon like Hoskins, I figure it's okay if I tell you. And I

47

couldn't think of anything else to write. But please, Mrs. Trumbley, do not tell anyone else this story!)

"I don't have it," I said. "I'd help you out, honest, if I could, but I lost it."

"Search him," said Hoskins, and Eddie made a move toward my pockets when we all heard the smack-smack of a grade seven girl jogging on pavement and Magnolia arrived in the nick of time.

"Sorry I'm late," she gasped between huffs. "I was waiting out front and it took a while to figure out where your whistle was coming from. Who're your friends?"

She stepped closer. "Oh, hi, Hoskins."

Hoskins let go of my arm and stepped back warily.

"It's the bean-girl. I told you about her," he said to Eddie.

"We'll continue this conversation another time," Eddie said to me and hurried Hoskins off toward the parking lot. I guess they didn't want Magnolia to know what they wanted.

I told Magnolia everything. "The only safe thing to do is to get the tooth back to the museum," I concluded. "Then Eddie will leave Dad and me alone and no one else will bother us either."

"Could you mail it back, without a note?" asked Magnolia.

"Maybe." I thought about it. "But how do we know whoever opens the envelope will really replace the tooth? They might keep it — or not recognize it and

48

throw it out. Or lose it. And we'll still have trouble with Eddie and Hoskins. It's only if it's really replaced and the papers carry the story that we'll be safe and left alone."

"Yeah. You're right. Let's try again tomorrow."

We took the bus to Magnolia's house; her parents were still up. Matilde was making some herb tea from herbs she'd collected and dried herself last summer — she had a *Recipees from the Middle Ages* book that told her how to do stuff like that. Harold of Dorcestor had his broken leg in a cast. He was sitting in an old-fashioned red high-back armchair and he rested the cast on a matching footstool. The house was nice and old. Lots of dark wood paneling half way up the walls and a beamed ceiling. Mom would love it — her chairs would feel right at home. Harold and Matilde had made a lot of their furniture themselves, all of it with a medieval look — dark wood armchairs with curled-down arms and decorations on the back. Matilde's tapestries on the wall were full of flowers and unicorns. There was a brown and white fur rug at one end of the room. Harold had a big heavy wood desk in the living room, and on it lay a quill pen and a pile of parchment. He saw me looking at it as we settled down for tea together.

"It's my new project," Harold explained. "The old manuscripts have always appealed to me, so I thought I'd learn how to make them. I've had the quills and parchment for a long time, but I've never been able to get to it. With this leg out of commission I'll have more time than I'll know what to do with, so Matilde brought it all up from the basement for me."

"Dad has stuff for a jillion projects in the basement," said Magnolia, rolling her eyes.

"My mother has chairs in ours," I said. Mom began to seem less weird to me. In fact, I was kind of proud of her. I thought Harold and Matilde and Mom would get along just fine.

"What are you going to write about?" asked Magnolia. "Armour and battles?"

"I'm not feeling too thrilled about all that," said Harold. "My leg hurts quite a lot you know... I thought I'd do something more peaceful. Birds maybe. Medicinal herbs." He was interrupted by a loud yawn from the fur rug. The rug stretched and heaved itself onto four spindly legs. The rug was a dog. It came up to my chest. It looked like it could eat most of me without even opening its mouth all the way.

"Don't worry," said Magnolia. "She doesn't bite. Her name is Yvonne. She's a Borzoi — that's a Russian wolfhound."

"Dogs," said Harold stretching out a hand to pat Yvonne. "That's what I'll do. A treatise on dogs of the Middle Ages."

It sounded good to me. Yvonne was a nice sloppy curly dog shaped like a crescent moon on its side, with a long pointing face and a tongue sort of like an ant-eater's when she licked you. She was very affectionate.

We went to sleep soon after that — the doctor had told Harold to get plenty of rest, and I was feeling pretty done in myself. I bunked down on the living room couch and Yvonne kept me company. She snored softly but it didn't keep me awake.

The next morning we all slept in and woke up about noon. Matilde suggested we go out to Sunday brunch at the Speedy Delight, a restaurant I'd never heard of. It sounded like fun, but Dad and I usually go to see the whales at the Aquarium on Sunday so I didn't think I could. Then Matilde called Mom and we all ended up going out for brunch and then on to the

whale show together. Mom, of course, had an antique wheelchair in the basement that fit Harold just fine.

✰ ✰ ✰ ✰ ✰ ✰ ✰

Speedy Delight did not turn out to be quite what I'd imagined. I'd thought it would be all bright chrome and plastic fluorescence, a hang-out with styrofoam plates and styrofoam food. Instead, Speedy Delight was down a flight of dark stairs and its sign was so unobtrusive I'd never have noticed it just walking by.

The restaurant itself was dark as a cave. The tables had checked tablecloths, red and white, and flowers, and a candle on every one, so it looked nice and there was enough candle-light to see by, but the light flickered and the shadows were terrific.

"This way to the bar," said Magnolia.

"We're not old enough to drink," I said.

"I mean the salad bar," said Magnolia.

Salad. I didn't really feel like salad.

"Do they have milkshakes here?" I asked.

"Really! You could be a little more adventurous, you know. You've had a million milkshakes. Why not try something new?"

"I like milkshakes. I know I like milkshakes. They're like old friends. Comfy. If I like milkshakes, what does it hurt?"

"They're on the far wall," Magnolia said with a small sigh. "Self-serve. You sure you don't want to stretch yourself a little? Maybe try a turnip-yam fizz?"

"You have the fizz," I said. "I'd like a chocolate milkshake."

Mrs. Trumbley, this was our first disagreement. It wasn't that serious, but it worried me a bit. Didn't Magnolia like me the way I was? How adventurous would I have to be?

I walked across the room. The wall was lined with little glass boxes holding all kinds of foods and drink. When you put coins in the slot, the glass door unlocked, and there was your food. Like a gigantic vending machine only with the most amazing selection. Warm boxes with clam curries and souffles and other entrees; cold boxes with desserts like chocolate mint yoghurt mousse — everything you could think of. Except chocolate milkshakes. I stretched myself. I got a cranberry yoghurt shake, fried artichoke supreme, and a truffle burger.

Matilde and Mom had heaping bowls of wild green salad and Harold had a caviar-and-squid omelette. Magnolia made two trips to the vending wall and came back with braised kiwi fruit and a quail-egg-and-boysenberry crepe. Dad opted for a casserole called Funky Noodles. We shared tastes and it was all fantastically delicious. And so speedy. Better than frozen — Mom loved it.

While we ate, there was a floor show — a man had

twelve trained white rats performing on a platform. The rats ran up ladders, opened hatches, walked tight-ropes and pulled strings that raised banners. It was a terrific show.

Everyone got along just fine, and after lunch we went to the whale show. Dad and I had watched the whales seventeen times this year alone — hundreds, probably, since I was born. There are three whales and a dolphin. The oldest one is Isador; the one with a sense of humour is Franz; Leonardo likes to keep to himself a bit, to think. Albert, the dolphin, likes to show off. I've watched the trainers here very carefully, and sometimes when they're not around, I stand at the pool's edge and give the little hand signals they use to get the whales to come, and bob, and swim in a circle, and breach, and things like that. Leonardo doesn't pay too much attention to me, but Franz usually comes along and has a good time slapping his tail and getting me wet. Then he goes off laughing. Like I say, he has a sense of humour. But I never mind — he doesn't do it to be mean. It's just his way of playing. I've practiced whale calls a lot — Dad has a record and lots of tapes and he and I actually both practice quite a bit (when Mom's not home) and when we get going, Franz will join in with this high-pitched squeal of his. I wish I knew what he was saying.

I didn't get the whales going myself this day because I didn't want everybody to get splashed. We just sat and watched the regular show, and it was as good as always. Those whales sure love their fish, and the trainers always have lots of fish to give them. They did this nice trick with a huge rubber ball, keeping it afloat with their nose and pushing it back to the trainer, just like they keep their calves up when the baby whale is newborn or if it gets injured, so they can breathe. Whales are naturally nice, I think.

''I wonder if they're happy, always doing the same old things,'' Magnolia mused.

''Of course they're happy. They wouldn't do them if they didn't like to,'' I said.

Somehow, Mrs. Trumbley, I don't think we were talking just about whales.

After the show we all went our separate ways. Harold needed to take a nap; Matilde wanted to work on a new tapestry. Mom had a chair to mend; Dad had taped the whale-show and was going to compare today's whale sounds with other tapes he had to see if any were similar enough to have a meaning. This is how he studies the whales' language.

Magnolia and I decided to go for a walk on the beach down by the golf course. We told our parents we'd be working on our English homework, thinking up ideas for our novels for you, Mrs. Trumbley.

The beach was nice — not too many people out but quite a few birds. Gulls mostly, a few sea-going ducks. The tide was low, and far out we could see a great blue heron looking like an elongated modern art statue on stilts. I was actually feeling pretty good. Here I was at the beach with a friend on a beautiful day. Life was fine. There was only one problem to attend to — returning the tooth to the museum. It was hard to think of other things like novel plots while that was on my mind. Magnolia must have been thinking the same thing.

"When should we try again with the tooth?" she asked.

"Well, Mom wouldn't want me to go out this evening after I was away all last night."

"I can see that, Duncan, but are you really thinking of your mom? Or are you getting cold feet? You know, this is your test, your quest. You can't turn back — you *must* return the tooth. And then you'll be a knight."

"I don't want to be a knight. Knights have to fight and either wind up dead or kill other knights. At the very least they get bones broken. I do want to return the tooth, but forget the knight business."

"Well, what are you going to do? Always stand on the sidelines and watch other people fight?"

"There's got to be a better way than fighting."

"That would be nice. But you can't always get a chocolate milkshake."

"No. Cranberry-yoghurt makes a nice change. But I still like chocolate. Maybe I can have both?"

"Food is food," said Magnolia. "Sometimes there are no milkshakes at all. Hoskins and Eddie are not milkshakes. What are you going to do about the tooth, throw it into the sea?"

I looked at the water, curling on the beach. "Don't tempt me.... No, I don't want to do that. Let me think."

I don't know, Mrs. Trumbley, why Magnolia and I were having these arguments. I guess we're different when it comes to problems. Maybe Magnolia likes to leap in and swim fast and hard when the water's cold and the waves are big. I prefer warm water and a gentle tide. If it's cold and rough, at least I like to go in slowly, get used to it bit by bit, bob around a little, tread water. Both ways are okay — neither of us will get smashed on the rocks. But she was right about one thing, I knew. You can't always stand on the sidelines.

"Look," I said, "Monday after supper I have my harmonica lesson and the music school's near the museum. This Monday, Mom and Dad are going to watch old movies at a friend's house. I can take the tooth back then."

"Could you get them to invite my parents?" Maggie asked. "Then I could come too."

"No problem," I said, "I hope."

# 7

There wasn't any problem. Our parents went off cheerfully to the movies on Monday after supper and Maggie and I took a bus across town. The bus was empty, which wasn't so strange since rush hour was long over, and we settled back to relax.

The bus wasn't making many of its regular stops, but I wasn't alarmed because the bus stops were empty. Every once in a while, it would stop to pick someone up, so I figured that maybe at night, buses didn't stop unless there was someone waiting or someone who wanted to get off.

After a while, the bus seemed to be taking a different route than usual.

"Should we get off?" asked Magnolia.

"We could try," I said. "But this is kind of fun. I'd sort of like to ride it out. At the end of his run, he'll turn around and bring us back."

"You're not just putting it off, are you Duncan? Sometimes you can't just go along for the ride."

"You said this was my quest — let me do it my way. I want to return the tooth *and* I want to see what happens with this bus. If you don't, I guess you could get off even if I stay on. You might miss something interesting, but that's up to you."

"I don't want to get off, I want you to be a knight."

"You want me to be your kind of knight. Maybe long ago there was only one kind. Maybe now there could be more than one kind."

"Maybe you're right, Duncan — I'll have to think about that. And no, I don't really want to get off the bus."

The people on the bus now were an odd assortment.

There was an older lady in a worn black coat and a huge purple hat with a heavy veil. You could hardly see her face. She carried two huge, heavily loaded shopping bags.

There was a dapper young man reading the *London*

*Times.* He wore a bowler hat and carried a black umbrella.

A girl in a green velvet jacket got on. She was carrying a large covered wicker basket from which came an occasional ''meow.''

The bus went through Chinatown, past bilingual street signs in Chinese and English, past apartment buildings with cupolas and restaurants strung with red lanterns.

We went through the East End, passing warehouses and derelict buildings which were gradually being converted into craft shops and artists' studios and Greek restaurants. Here the bus stopped and picked up two Greek sailors carrying the *London Times.*

I saw the Purple Hat lady's face move. It was hard to tell, but I think she was smiling. She fished around in one of her bags and took out a loaf of rye bread, some cheese, a knife and her copy of the *London Times.*

The girl in the green velvet jacket, sitting across from the bag lady, opened her basket a crack, patted her cat, and extracted her copy of the *London Times.*

''Is anybody hungry?'' called out the Purple Hat. ''Here's food enough for everybody!'' Her voice sounded familiar.

I hadn't eaten much for supper and I suddenly realized I was famished.

''I'm starving,'' I said to Magnolia. ''Do you happen to have our copy of the *London Times?*''

''Nope,'' she said, ''forgot it.''

63

"It happens," said the Purple Hat, who must have overheard us. "Come and eat."

Everyone changed seats to form a kind of picnic group. The Greek sailors produced some black olives as wrinkled as if they'd been soaking in a long bath. The Green Velvet Jacket produced a bag of green grapes from her basket. Dapperman chipped in a chocolate bar. The driver must have noticed the picnic preparations in his mirror. He stopped the bus just long enough to bring back some paper cups and a bottle of pineapple juice.

I turned to Magnolia.

"Did we bring anything?" I asked. "Or did we forget that too?"

"Will bubblegum do?" Magnolia asked. "I usually have some bubblegum in case of emergencies."

"Bubblegum will be nice," said the Purple Hat.

The food was passed around and everyone took some of everything. It all tasted terrific.

"Let's sing!" said Dapperman.

One of the Greek sailors took out shepherd's pipes and played while everybody sang "The Spare Went Over the Mountain" and "Found a Gecko." I played along on my harmonica.

Then the sailor played a solo. Maybe it was a Greek song. It was beautiful, in a minor key — haunting and a bit sad. Then he played a jolly fast one and the other sailor tried to dance in the aisle, but it didn't work well with the bus moving so he fell back into his seat laughing.

We hadn't made a stop for a long time, nor had I been watching out the window.

When I looked, we were out in the country. It was dark and hard to see anything but trees and cleared areas that must have been fields. Now and then we passed a farm house with a light still on. Finally, we turned off the road onto a long winding driveway that led to a huge old house.

The bus stopped and everybody got up to get out. The bus driver got out first and stood by the steps to help everybody down.

"What now?" asked Magnolia.

"Beats me," I said.

Everybody else, including the bus driver, was heading toward the house. I couldn't see a bus stop sign.

The Purple Hat was bringing up the rear. She turned and called back to us, "Hurry up, you two. Can't keep the Colonel waiting."

"Are you game?" Magnolia asked.

"No, let's go back. This might take too long."

"If we don't go in, we'll never know what this is all about. Besides, it's better than walking back — if we go in, we might get a ride."

"Okay. This time we'll go along for the ride."

Magnolia gave me a funny look. "Score one for your side," she said and laughed.

The house was a mansion. Huge, open stone fire-

place, high ceilings, gleaming oak floors, dark leather couches and delicate chairs with white satin seats and curved backs. Mom would have loved the chairs.

A butler took our coats and hats and told us to sit down, saying, ''The Colonel will be with you soon.''

Several dogs, large and small, lay snoozing before the fireplace. And before long, the Colonel came in and stood beside the dogs, his hands behind his back. He was short and had a handlebar mustache. He wore a tweed suit with a vest and a gold watch chain.

''Welcome,'' he said, ''welcome one and all. I'm glad you've all decided to answer the advert I placed in the *Times*. You're all right on time, and a fine looking team you are too.''

''Excuse me,'' I said. ''But I've forgotten my copy of the *Times* and my friend here hasn't seen the advert yet. Could we have a copy, please?''

''Certainly,'' said the Colonel, taking a copy of the *London Times* from a magazine rack and opening it to the Personal column. He pointed out a small square.

It said: ''For Adventurous Spirits Only — WAR GAMES — Team members needed by Colonel H. T. Sprott, 8 p.m. April 2nd, Ruxton Hall. Wait at Route No. 98 bus stops for transportation.''

''Thank you,'' I said.

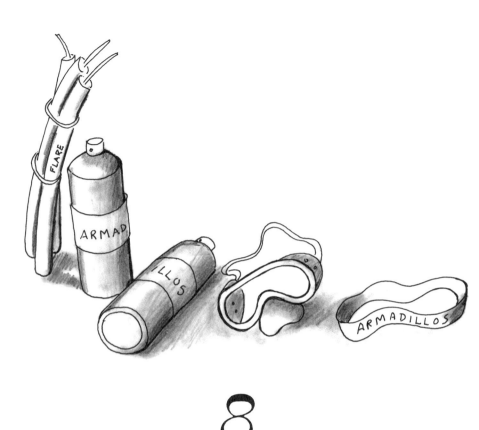

"Unreal," said Magnolia. (You may be thinking the same thing, Mrs. Trumbley. You had to be there.) The Colonel passed out protective face masks, flares for emergencies, and spray cans of white paint. The object was to spray the enemy before he sprayed you. We were given maps of an obstacle course marked with hiding places, open areas, and rendezvous points. Our code name was Armadillo. We were after the Ostrich team organizing two farms away. They would have spray cans of yellow paint. We were supposed to try not to spray-paint members of our own team, but if we did, the colours would be different so the other team couldn't get extra points.

The Ostriches were wearing flourescent pink head bands. Armadillo heads glowed a lime green.

"Before we start," announced the Colonel, "I'd like to tell you about a little tour I'm planning for next Christmas. It's called "War Zones Around the World." We'll holiday in Central America, the Middle East — anywhere that looks like fun. Escape the cold, I always say — come to the hot spots. Anyone who's interested can see me after the game. And now it's time to begin. On your mark, get ready, get set, go!" The Colonel fired a blank from a starting pistol and we went.

Out the door, down the driveway, across the street and into the brush we trotted, our team fanning out.

"Stay close," Magnolia whispered to me.

"Don't worry, I will."

I spotted a large tree and behind it found a hollow hidden by shrubbery. Magnolia and I stopped.

"What do you think we should do?" she asked.

I was pleased. Magnolia the brave, Magnolia the warrior knight, my friend Magnolia was asking me what to do.

"The way I see it," I said, "we have a couple of choices. We can play out the war game. We can try walking back to sanity and phone our parents from a farmhouse. We can sleep here under the stars tonight and try phoning or hitching home in the morning. We can go back to the house and tell the Colonel we don't want to play, use his phone, etc. Have I missed out anything?''

''I don't think so,'' said Magnolia.

I thought of calling Dad and asking him to try using the table to get us home, but I didn't know exactly where we were. He was getting better, but it would be foolish to ask him to try a setting he wasn't familiar with. He had talent, I had to admit, but there were limits.

''Well?'' I asked.

''I can't decide,'' said Magnolia. ''I'm good until tomorrow around noon. Then I'll just drop, wherever I am.''

''Me too,'' I said. I put my hands in my pocket and remembered the tooth.

''There's one thing,'' I said. ''I still have to get the tooth back, preferably before tomorrow morning. I think we should probably skip the war tonight and concentrate on the tooth. Besides, do you really want to play war?''

''No,'' said Magnolia. ''You're right. They're fighting because they like it. Nothing's dumber than that.''

We turned back to the mansion to explain we were pacifists and needed to use the phone, but the door was locked and no one answered the bell.

"Down the road?" I suggested.

"Down the road," Magnolia said.

We got about to the edge of the driveway when we were distracted by a flare going off to the right.

"What does that mean?" Magnolia asked.

"I'm not sure. It's either marking a kill or asking for help."

"How could it be asking for help? Everybody can see it — we don't even know what team it's from. If both teams answer it, whoever threw the flare will inevitably be killed or wounded by the enemy."

"Same thing happens in a real war, I guess. If someone's really in enough trouble to risk sending up a flare, we'd better go see if we can help," I decided. "There'd be no point in marking a kill with a flare."

"I know," Magnolia said. "Let's go. The worst that can happen is we'll be spray-painted by an Ostrich."

"Or by an Armadillo, by mistake. Do armadillos often make mistakes?" I asked.

"Only when they're over-excited and are carrying spray-cans of paint. Hadn't we better be quiet? Or do you care if we're painted?"

"I don't much care if we're painted," I said. "But if that flare means something really complicated and troublesome is going on, maybe we'd better not attract other people until we figure out what's up."

Magnolia and I settled down to business, using our stealthiest creep-through-the-tropical-jungles technique, until we reached the clearing where we thought we'd seen the flare go up. We found the remains of the flare, but no person.

"Pssst?" I tried in a hoarse whisper. "Anybody home? If you're in trouble, we'll try to help, no matter what team you're on."

"What are you, a MASH unit? I'm caught up here." The answering whisper came from above.

Magnolia and I took a minute to make out the net suspended high in the cedar branches. Inside the net was the Purple Hat.

"Don't worry, we'll get you down," I said.

"Make it fast," the Purple Hat returned. "I don't want to miss any of the action."

"The lowest branch is too high to reach, even if I give you a leg up," said Magnolia. "How are we going to get up the tree to get her down?"

"I'm not sure — that is one high net. How are you at flying?"

"Shhh!"

There were noises coming from the woods — we weren't the only ones to spot the flare.

"Do we spray first and ask questions later?" Magnolia asked.

"Let's try doing this without spilling a drop of paint," I said. "As an experiment."

I capped my can. Then I said out loud, "Halt and hands up! I've got you covered!"

It was an Ostrich, I could tell from the headband. A very, very tall Ostrich, tall enough to take a running leap and catch hold of the lowest branch.

"Here's the deal, Ostrich," Magnolia said, the way they talk on T.V. "You climb the tree and help our friend down, and we'll let you get away unpainted. Any funny business and we'll spray. Understand?"

"Sure thing. Stay cool. I can dig it." The very tall Ostrich took a running leap, climbed the tree and released the Purple Hat.

I thought, when the lady got back to ground level, she would need a doctor, at worst, or at least a little time to catch her breath.

"Nonsense," she said, shocked and insulted when I suggested we could sit with her for awhile. "What do you take me for, a novice? I've been through more campaigns than you can count! I know my way around, I can tell you, and I've had all the rest I need in that there hammock. Now where's that Ostrich? Let me at him!"

But the Ostrich had deftly faded back into the under-brush during the Purple Hat's tirade.

"What we need is a little cheer to get our spirits up," said the Purple Hat, and she went into a cheer-leader's routine:

*Gimme an arm —*
*Arm!*
*Gimme an ah —*
*Ah!*
*Gimme a dill —*
*Dill!*

*Gimme an oh —*
            *Oh!*
*Armadillo, armadillo*
*Go, Go, Go!*

And then:
*Fee, fi, forward fumble*
*I'm in the mood for a Grade A rumble!*
*Sigma Pi, Sigma Shoo,*
*War games are what's good for you!*
*A, B, C, D, E, F, G —*
*Let's have a cheer for VICTORY!''*

Magnolia and I left. The Purple Hat probably spent the rest of the night doing cheers. Her voice still sounded familiar but I couldn't quite place it.

''This way?'' Magnolia suggested, taking the lead. All ways looked the same to me, so I was glad to follow. I felt in my pocket — the tooth was still there and so was my harmonica. I figured all we needed was a regular commercial bus headed toward the city, and I might even beat my parents home.

I figured without Eddie.

''Halt!'' a familiar voice growled from the shrubbery.

Magnolia and I halted.

A red-headed Ostrich emerged from the underbrush, complete with his junior sidekick, Hoskins, who grabbed Magnolia and held her in a half nelson. They were armed with paint cans and were aiming them at Magnolia's face.

"What are you doing here?" I blurted.

"We've been following you two," said Eddie. "When we saw you hop the bus, we took a cab and followed it. While we were waiting for you to come out of the big house, an Ostrich told us what was going on and we joined up. Thought it would be fun to play with you, Duncan."

Un huh.

"Now give us the tooth or we'll paint your girlfriend!" Hoskins snarled.

"Run!" yelled Magnolia bravely.

I didn't stop to argue whether Magnolia was my girlfriend or not — I reached in my pocket and found my harmonica. So far, so good. I guess I should have been too scared to move, but I didn't have time for that. I whirled quickly and threw it as hard as I could— it made a sound landing in the brush very like a large tooth might.

Hoskins and Eddie both turned to look and that gave me enough time to set off a flare. Before long, we all knew we'd have company.

"Did you see where it went?" Eddie asked Hoskins.

"Sounded like to the left, near that big oak," Hoskins said.

"Come on, you young twerp," Eddie said to me. "You're gonna find it yourself."

But just as he made a lunge for me, we were joined by Green Jacket, wearing her cat on her shoulder, and Dapperman.

77

"I say," said Dapperman, "you've made a fine Ostrich capture here. We'll take these two prisoners along to camp. Come on, you two."

I didn't know what would happen to Eddie and Hoskins at camp, and I didn't care. I wasn't all that surprised to see them here, actually. War games are about the only games creeps like Hoskins and Eddie play.

9

We walked almost forever until we could catch a bus. The rest of the trip home was not too eventful, except for Magnolia apologizing: "That was quick thinking, quick throwing. Like a true and noble knight."

"Thanks," I said, "but I really don't think I'm knight-material."

Magnolia smiled. "I think you are," she said.

I found our key where Mom always hid it under

an apple box filled with driftwood to the left of the door. Now and then we even used a stick of wood for the fireplace, but most of it was there for carving. Mom collected interesting pieces in case she ever wanted to get into polishing and carving driftwood. She'd never actually gone that far, but she liked collecting it. She even had a chainsaw for large pieces.

Mom and Dad were asleep. I knew that Hoskins and Eddie would be after us as soon as they could get away. Possibly they would be catching the next bus. Or, if they hitched a ride, they might get home even faster. I didn't think I should try waiting any longer to return the tooth to the museum myself. The best way would be to send it back tonight and I needed Dad for that.

Magnolia agreed. "But how shall we wake them up?" she asked.

"Waking them is not much of a problem," I said. "Waking them so they're in a good mood is the problem."

"Who's there?" said my mother from the bedroom. She must have heard us talking.

"It's us — Duncan and Magnolia," I answered.

"What is it? You're getting married or something? You're too young to get married! Wake up, Benjamin. Duncan and Magnolia are getting married and they're too young." I could hear Dad and Mom bustling about, getting into bathrobes and slippers.

"We're not even holding hands," I tried, but when

Mom gets an idea into her head, it's hard to shake.

"Don't get married. Listen to me. You're too young, you'll regret it. I'm not coming out there until you promise you'll listen to your mother!"

"Okay," I said, "we won't get married. We've thought better of it. You've convinced us. I promise. Magnolia promises. We will not get married. Now will you come out and talk with us?"

"Now I will go back to bed," my mother said. "If you're not getting married, we can talk in the morning."

"Mom, please! This is important! If you don't come, we'll get married!"

"Okay, I'll come. I'll come."

Mom made some coffee and popped some frozen Shredded Webbies in the toaster and Dad settled himself to listen.

"Well?" he asked. "What's new?"

"Dad, are you awake or not? It is I, Duncan, your son, come home with the you-know-what."

"I was trying to be subtle," said Dad. "Your mom doesn't know about the you-know-what."

Just as I'd thought.

"Dad, we have to get the tooth back right away."

"I know, I know. We'll take it over to Eddie's and I'll send it back."

"There's one little complication I'm afraid you don't know about. Eddie wants to keep the tooth. Himself."

81

"So what's new about that? Eddie wants to keep everything himself. Remember last year, he took a vacation in the Northwest Territories? He wanted to keep the Northwest Territories himself. We'll just tell him no. The tooth has to go back."

"Dad, this is different. He's getting really nasty. He and Hoskins have been threatening us."

"Look, Duncan, you stay here with your mother and I'll go talk to Eddie. I'll make him see reason."

"Who wants a Shredded Webby?" asked my mother, coming into the room with a plateful.

"I have to go talk to Eddie," said Dad. "You stay and eat."

Magnolia and Mom and I ate Shredded Webbies. They're actually quite good — honey and nuts — it's just the name that's a bit disgusting. They also come in cinnamon and chocolate-mint. They're not at all bad even if they are frozen.

After a while, Dad came back. "Eddie won't talk to me alone," he said. "He wants to see you, Duncan, with the tooth."

"What are you two talking about?" asked Mom. "What tooth? What about talking with Eddie in the middle of the night? You have a tooth-ache, Duncan? Can't your own dad fix it for you?"

"Mom, we didn't tell you before because we didn't want you to worry, but we probably have to tell you now."

"So? Tell."

"Remember the pineapple that Dad disappeared with the table?"

"Sure, I remember the pineapple. It was still a little green."

"Well, I found the pineapple in the museum, in the place of a medieval relic, the alleged Tooth of Saint Anthony. The tooth disappeared, but to keep this story as short and as clear as possible, Magnolia and I found the missing tooth in a fish. I know it sounds confusing. Maybe you had to be there. We've been trying to return the tooth, one way or another, to the museum collection. The best way would be for Dad to exchange it for the pineapple using the table, the way he did before, but the other way around."

"So? Go ahead. Exchange it. What's the problem?"

"Eddie is the problem, Mom. Eddie wants to keep the tooth himself, for a trophy. He and Hoskins have been trying to get it away from us."

"And did they?"

"No. We still have the tooth. But Eddie won't let us send it back."

"You're going to have to do something about Eddie and his business associate," said my mom. "Think, Duncan, think."

I thought. Bribe them with Shredded Webbies? I doubted it. Pull out one of our teeth and try to palm it off as the relic? Eddie was a dentist; he'd know the difference.

If we had big-game tranquilizer guns, we could put

them to sleep long enough to use the table, and they would wake up unhurt. But we didn't have big-game tranquilizer guns. If we had the right kind of net, we could tangle them up and hold them fast while we used the table, but we didn't have the right kind of net. There should be some kind of foam that would stun them and immobilize them but do no permanent damage... This was silly. Fantasies wouldn't get us anywhere. We had to be practical.

"The answer has to be something we have around the house," I said. "Something common and obvious, that we're just not thinking of."

"I could break the washing machine so it overflows suds, but it won't make enough to get next door," said Mom.

"That's the right kind of thinking, Mom, keep going."

"It probably wouldn't even make enough suds to give the chairs a good washing."

"Never mind," I said.

"I wish I had my baked beans thermos," said Magnolia, "but it probably wouldn't work twice on the same person. Maybe we could bribe them? Is there anything Eddie and Hoskins especially like?"

"Teeth," I muttered, "but I'd like to keep mine.... I'm kind of attached to them. Wait a minute! There *is* something... Maggie, you're a genius! You've got it!"

"So?" asked Mom and Dad.

"What did I get?" asked Magnolia.

"Break-dancing! Eddie and Hoskins love break-dancing to crazy loud music!"

Magnolia looked thoughtful. "Do we have any crazy loud music?" she asked.

"We have whale songs," said Dad. "I could turn the volume up."

"Perfect!" I said. "And Mom, we'll need your chain saw."

"Yes, sir!" Mom said happily and brought the saw while Dad set his loudest whale tap in his tape-deck.

"Now here's what we'll do — we'll come in playing the whale songs and the chain saw, break-dancing like crazy and while we have them off-guard, one of us will send the tooth back."

"What's this break-dancing?" asked Mom.

"I can't let this whale tape out of my hands," said Dad. "I'll tell you how to send the tooth back."

"Could someone tell me how to do this dancing?" asked Mom.

For a minute I was stuck. If there's one thing I can't do, it's break-dancing. Would the whole beautiful scheme collapse? It looked like we'd never find a way....

Then Magnolia piped up. "I think I can break-dance," she said. "I've never tried, but...turn on the music?"

Well, we had a first-rate rehersal! Magnolia was a champion at flips and flings. Mom did her own sort of dance — something like imitating an airplane. Dad did aerobic kicks and push-ups — it was grand!

Dad told me how to work the laser table and it didn't sound too hard. We were ready.

We all trooped over to Eddie's house. Hoskins was watching an old war movie on T.V. When he saw Magnolia and me, his eyes flashed evilly, but when Dad and Mom walked in behind us, he went back to his lazy lizard look. There were explosion sounds coming from the T.V. and the picture was of all kinds of stuff blowing up — pieces of wood and bricks sent flying — I've seen that shot in every war movie I've ever turned off on T.V. In the real thing, there'd be skin and eyeballs too.

"I want the tooth back," Eddie whined.

"I'm sorry, Eddie," said my dad, taking Eddie's arm.

Mom took his other arm. "Sit down a while with us, Eddie dear," she said. "Come and meet Magnolia."

"We've met," said Maggie.

"Ready, set, play!" I said. I was feeling pretty scared and my voice cracked, but Dad flicked on the whales and Mom's chain-saw roared into action. Dad did his kicks and push-ups, Mom whirled like a jet-dervish, and Magnolia flipped and flung magnificently. Eddie and Hoskins were struck dumb, hypnotized, stupified — they barely blinked, stared open-mouthed, and then, as if pulled by a hidden force, they began, clumsily, to join in the dance.

While all this was going one, I slipped downstairs to the basement. I took the tooth to the table, set it in

position, aimed the controls, pressed the buttons, and zappo! I'd done it! I hadn't been sure I could — it was just a last ditch attempt — but I'd really done it! The tooth was gone and in the middle of the table sat the pineapple named Duncan and a small something else, both of which I carred upstairs.

When I appeared, Dad stopped the music. Eddie stared at me in shock, then slumped into a chair.

"It's gone," said Eddie, sadly. "And now there's no trophy at all. Not even a souvenir."

He looked as if he would break into sobs any minute.

"There, there," I said. "It's not so bad, Eddie. I made a souvenir for you. Look."

I gave him the small plastic hologram of the tooth.

Eddie gazed at the hologram. Then he smiled a little; finally, he spoke.

"Thanks," he said. "I'll always treasure this."

When we left Eddie's, Hoskins was playing a video game called Missile Madness. I've seen it before. In this game, global powers keep getting more and more nuclear missiles and your player has to keep destroying the missiles, catching them in mid-flight sometimes when one of the countries has an accident and lets loose a warhead. Sometimes, a peaceful protest will knock off a missile, if your player can draw a ring around the missile without being intercepted by Security Guards. If you lose, there's lots of flashing lights, loud noises, firestorms, etc.

I haven't seen anyone win it yet.

Dad drove Magnolia home and I went to bed. I felt like I could sleep for a hundred years.

Just before she left, I asked Magnolia if she knew what Saint Anthony was the saint of.

"Sure," she said. "Saint Anthony of Padua — he's the patron saint of lost or stolen articles."

"Of course," I said.

"Of course," said Magnolia. "And you sent the tooth back — you have completed your task and passed your test." She paused, picked an umbrella out of the stand by our front door, and turned to face me. "Kneel, please."

It seemed kind of nuts but I didn't feel like arguing. I knelt.

Magnolia touched me lightly on the shoulder with the umbrella and said, "I dub thee Sir Duncan. You are now a knight. Rise, Sir Duncan."

I rose, shaking my head. I hadn't wanted to be a knight, but Fate is funny. Maybe, Mrs. Trumbley, there *is* more than one kind of knight.

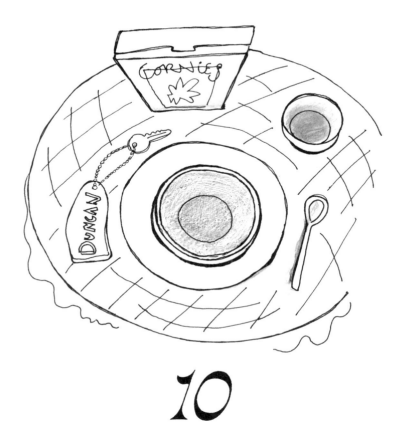

# 10

The next day was Tuesday. When I woke at seven, Dad had already dismantled the table — he knew Eddie wouldn't be able to get it back to a dematerializing state by himself, and as far as Dad was concerned, he'd had enough of that for a while.

"Some time I'll come back to it," he said. "Not now. But some time. There are still a few rough edges I need to polish up."

I found my lucky key-ring name-tag at my plate on the dining room table. We had pineapple for breakfast. By now, it was ripe.

When I got to school, I could see a circle of kids on the playground, like there usually was around Hoskins and whoever he was picking on. Sometimes, I wondered if he paid some of those kids to stand in a circle and watch, just to keep the old public image up. I elbowed my way through the crowd to the front row, to see if whatever was going on needed stopping, and what I could do about it.

There in the centre, as I'd suspected, was Hoskins, and the kid he was badgering couldn't have been more than five or six.

"Pay your dues to the club or something terrible could happen to you," said Hoskins.

"But I don't have any money," said the kid. "You took my whole allowance for the week yesterday. I don't get any more 'til next Sunday." I could tell he was near tears.

Where was Magnolia, I wondered. She would know what to do, how to stop this. But I couldn't see her anywhere. Hoskins was looking more and more fierce and the little guy was beginning to sob. I knew that this time, it was completely up to me.

"Stop!" I tried to say, but my tongue got all twisted and it came out more like "Shlop!" It didn't matter too much — I'd meant to shout but it came out so low nobody could hear anyway.

I had to try again.

"Leave him alone, Hoskins," I said, walking into the middle of the circle. My voice cracked but I knew I had to go on. "Pick on someone your own size."

I was surprised at myself, butting right in that way. But it began to feel all right. Good, even. In this life you have to take chances. Like Magnolia's baked beans. I wondered if she was in the crowd watching.

"Well, look who's here," said Hoskins, "the tooth fairy. Are you gonna pay what that kid owes me?"

"No," I said. "But you'll have to beat me up before you get to him."

"No sweat," said Hoskins. "Put up your dukes." He was holding up his fists like a boxer and dancing back and forth on the balls of his feet. I knew he'd cream me. I was beginning to feel this was one of the dumber things I'd done. But I'd started it, and I meant to finish it. I was even a little curious about how it would come out in the end.

"I'm not going to fight you," I said in my calmest, most non-violent voice. "I'm just going to stay between you and the kid until either you go away or you put me away."

"Yellow belly!" sneered Hoskins.

"It's not especially brave to beat up little kids," I said. "Why don't you just drop it and go on in? The bell's going to ring any minute."

"So why don't you go, yellow belly?"

"I'm staying until this is settled," I said, wondering

93

if the crowd of kids would disappear when the bell rang, and what Hoskins would do to me when they did.

The bell did go and a few kids did vault the steps into the building, but a hefty number stayed with us on the playground.

"Okay," said Hoskins, "If you want to get beat up, I'll grant your wish." And he looked like he really was hauling back to sock me.

I gritted my teeth and fought a terrific impulse to close my eyes.

"You'll have to beat me up, too," said a voice behind me. I looked around — it was a chubby kid with braces.

"And me!"

"Me too!"

Everyone was joining in — I heard Magnolia's voice somewhere in the crowd. It was fantastic — our own non-violent resistence movement. I couldn't believe it. And what's more, it worked!

"Aw, nuts," muttered Hoskins, and he moved off, pretending to saunter, right out of the school yard.

Then everyone was cheering and laughing and clapping each other on the back and we went into the school. And that really was the end of Hoskins' bullying in the schoolyard. He's probably just as evil as ever if he gets somebody alone somewhere, but if there's more than one of us, we know what to do.

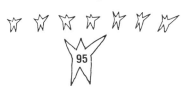

I still had this novel to write for you, Mrs. Trumbley. First I made up a regular story about a poor little orphan boy who got a job in a toothpick factory. At first everyone was mean to him and he didn't get enough to eat and the story was very sad. But then he worked so hard and was so honest and virtuous that the president of the toothpick company adopted him and he gave him a lot of shares in the company.

The boy kept on working hard and invented curved toothpicks for hard-to-fit mouths, and his father, who was the president, said, "My son, it is time for you to take my place." And the son became president of the company and he gave his father lots of shares and lots of curvy toothpicks, some with double twists.

It was a pretty good story, I thought, but it was hard to write, because, for a few parts anyway, I'd never been there.

So I wrote this novel instead, about my recent life. I hope you like it, Mrs. Trumbley. If you don't, well, maybe you had to be there.

P.S. Do you happen to own a purple hat?